CHIMES
FOR
CHILDREN

Written & drawn by Nicolas Hill

Chimes for Children

Stacey International
128 Kensington Church Street
London W8 4BH
Tel: 020 7221 7166 Fax: 020 7792 9288
website: www.stacey-international.co.uk
e-mail: marketing@stacey-international.co.uk

ISBN: 978-1-906768-13-3

CIP Data: A catalogue record for this book is available from the British Library

Written and illustrated by Nicolas Hill

Photograph by Damian Risdon

Printed in China

CONTENTS

For Pamela Idelson
and her daughter Zara

The King and the Moon

The moon fell down from the midnight sky
And hit the King as he passed by.
"You silly moon," the cross King said,
"How dare you hurt my royal head."

Little Cloud

During a dark and dismal day
A little cloud that lost its way
Said to a policeman passing by,
"Please can you help me find the sky?"

The Wasp

A dandy wasp is Billy Brown,
He's such a lad when he's in town,
With stripy suit and well-pressed wings,
But girls watch out! He often stings.

Roast Fly

At Christmas when the snow flakes fall
And peace on earth is wished for all
My friends and I we like to try
A plump and nicely roasted fly.

The Faery Shop

There is a shop (so I am told)
Where only faery things are sold
Like dew drop sweets and petal shoes
And every day the Faery News.

The Wizard

The Wizard is a wonderous man
Who fries his jelly in a pan
And turns fish fingers into mice
And makes balloons from bags of rice.

Laughs with a Giraffe

Should you by chance meet a giraffe
And want to share a jolly laugh
But find the fellow's head too high
Just pop him in a well nearby.

Peas in a Pod

The peas they thought it very odd
To spend their lives inside a pod.
So once upon a summer's day
They all climbed out to dance and play.

Alphonse

My Alphonse is a teddy bear
Who lost his eye and half an ear
But when at night the witches ride
I love to have him by my side.

The Mermaid

When sailing with a bearded goat
Aboard a steam-powered paddle boat
We both saw sitting by the sea
A lovely mermaid drinking tea.

King Bun the Bad

King Bun the Bad was holding court
As knightly buns in armour fought.
They fought and fought till they were stale
And that is the end of this short tale.

Napoleon

With hidden hand and studied frown
Napoleon marched on Moscow town.
When Moscow burnt and winter came
Napoleon then marched back again.

The Butterfly

I'd love to be a butterfly,
And drift about the summer sky
To gently flit from flower to flower,
Enjoying every sunny hour.

Mr and Mrs Shark

Said Mr Shark, "There's going to be
A Tesco built beneath the sea
Where we can purchase all our needs
Including prunes and seaweed seeds."

Our Garden Gnome

I cannot say I'm very fond
Of that old gnome by our fish pond.
You see he fishes day and night
And never once has had a bite.

Noah's Ark

Said Neemah to Noah, "What is that?"
"Dear wife," he answered, "That's a rat."
"Noah," she screamed, "go tell the Lord,
I'm not having no rats aboard."

Fly Agaric

Dear children never, never pick
A toadstool known as Fly Agaric.
This fiendish fungus has the power
To kill you off within an hour.

The Rainbow

You'll never find the rainbow's end
Or paint it red or mend its bend
Or take it home for Mum to see
Or eat it with baked beans for tea.

The Old Queen

One day the Old Queen lost her crown,
"Oh drat," she muttered with a frown,
The Queen then looked beneath her bed
And found the crown was on her head.

Tears in a Bath

To fill a bath with only tears
Would take a person many years.
Miranda once said she would try
But couldn't even drown a fly.

The Tortoise and the Hare

The Hare and Tortoise had a race,
The Hare went at a furious pace
And when he won the Tortoise cried,
"Old Aesop was a fraud: he lied."

The Tramp and the Duke

The Tramp said to his friend the Duke,
"Our lives are just a funny fluke.
You dine on lobster, grouse and quince
While I'm too poor to buy some mince."

The Stars at Day

Where do the stars go in the day?
The goose said they are put away
Into a bag that's red and brown
By an ancient man in a dressing gown.

Cinderella

Poor Cinders now has got the gout,
You see she's old and rather stout.
But still she grabs at every chance
To go with Charming to a dance.

If I had a Maid

If I had a maid, you could stay!
A maid to do the chores all day,
To make the beds to cook a hen,
A maid to wait on gentlemen.

The White-faced Man

The white-faced man is rather queer.
He lives his life upon a deer
And from its horns he hangs his razor,
Bag of food and pink striped blazer.

Swallowtail

I once saw by an upturned pail
A bright and lovely Swallowtail.
I've looked and looked but all in vain
For I never saw its like again.

Humpty Dumpty

Humpty Dumpty was overweight,
(The reason was he ate and ate).
The doctor said, "Get off that wall,
And jog before you have a fall."

Lord Nelson

Although he only had one eye
Lord Nelson liked to play I-Spy.
"Look lads, I-Spy the French," he cried.
That's sadly when our hero died.

Dunwich

At Dunwich where there used to be
A town that's now beneath the sea,
You still can hear the ghostly sound
As church bells ring for sailors drowned.

The Bishop's Wife

The Bishop's wife had such a fright.
It happened on a Sunday night
When from the china soup tureen
Out leapt a frog of brightest green.

The Cow

The cow when munching lots of grass
Said to a fly that chanced to pass,
"Who blows the wind? Who makes the snow?
And where do all the raindrops go?"

End Poem

The sun is out and I am old
So children do as you are told
While I shall end these chimes of mine
And drink a welcome glass of wine.

THE END